LISAMARIE KADE

one

. . .

"Come on, Marina! It's damn cold. You can stare at him from inside, through the window." I point to the glass doors of Gravity Ski Hill.

"Fine, fine. Call me a stalker, but I am gonna stare until that fine-ass specimen is out of sight."

I roll my eyes as we grab a seat by the window. It gives us the perfect view of the guy Marina is currently scoping out.

"That's better," she says.

I sit back and take my gloves off. We haven't even been in Breckenridge for three hours and my best friend has already found a piece of eye candy.

I scroll my phone mindlessly to pass the time. Our room isn't ready yet. We went out to grab a bite and upon returning, she spotted Mr. Tall, Dark, and Handsome.

Now here we are.

"Oh my God, Callia. He looked at me. Like looked at me and smiled."

Glancing up from my phone, I see Marina blushing. I shake my head. "You are crazy."

"Maybe, but you put up with me."

"This is true," I say as my cell phone vibrates in my hand. A text message from the resort lets me know our room is finally ready.

"Room is ready, let's go."

As soon as I head for the front desk, Marina and I cross paths with the guy she's been ogling. I'll admit, he is good looking. Dark wavy hair. Eyes that are as black as the night sky. He's tall, and it is clear that he works out. He looks like the dream package.

"Hello, ladies."

Holy hell. Even his deep voice sounds hot. I smile and keep walking because as soon as I hear Marina say hello from behind me, I know that she has stopped. I don't even hear her feet.

When I reach the counter, I turn to look back at my friend. Her cheeks are red and her smile is so bright. The two of them are lost in conversation. It's almost like one of those romantic holiday movies.

Ugh. Makes me want to gag. I'm not bitter or jealous. I'm just anti-love right now. I have no desire to date after my last disaster of a relationship.

By the time I finish with the check-in process, Marina and the guy are sitting together in a love seat that is sectioned in the middle of the lobby. People pass them as they come and go from the resort. It really does feel like they are on the set of a movie.

The two of them are so lost in conversation that neither of them notice when I approach. I have to clear my throat to get their attention.

"Oh hey, Callia," Marina says with a giant smile on her face. "This is Leon. Leon, this is my best friend, Callia."

He stands and just when I stick my hand out, thinking he wants to shake it, he pulls me in for a hug and kisses me on the cheek.

Well, okay then.

I take a step back, smiling. That's the polite thing to do, right? It must be because Leon smiles back before taking his seat again.

"It is a pleasure to meet you." Damn, what a sexy accent he has.

"Leon is here on holiday," Marina says, and he nods with that smile still plastered on his face. One thing is clear. He is a charmer.

"Our room is ready." I hold up the little envelope that holds our room keys.

"It's about time!" Marina claps her hands as she climbs to her feet. "Oh, um, Leon. Maybe we can grab a drink or something later?"

I stare at my best friend. I see a sparkle of hope in her piercing green eyes. I go to speak up, you know to remind her that this is a girls trip. Before I can get a single syllable out, Leon is on his feet, taking Marina's hands in his.

"What about your plans with your friend?"

"Callia will be fine. We don't have any plans tonight. Right, Callia?" Maria gives me her best puppy dog eyes. The ones she knows I can never say no to.

"She's right. We don't have anything going on this evening. You two should go and get drinks down in the lounge later."

"Perfect. Say six o'clock? I'll be at the bar. Waiting." His damn voice is mesmerizing.

"I'll be there."

Leon kisses Marina's hand before leaving us alone.

"Marina!" I half whisper on the way to find our room.

"I know! I know. I owe you."

I shake my head. She owes me all right.

two

. . .

"How do I look?" Marina asks as she fluffs her dark hair in the hotel room mirror.

She stands there in a pair of jeans and red knit sweater that has a matching knit headband. Fluffy boots cover her feet. She oozes beauty and confidence. I consider myself pretty, beautiful even, but could use a little boost in the confidence department. I owe that all to my ex-boyfriend. He really did a number on my ego. Cheating on me and all that crap.

"You look fine," I reply while rolling my eyes. "Besides, it's not like you are wearing some sexy outfit. We're in Breckenridge, and it's cold."

"So, I still need to look good for Leon."

I shake my head while she dabs lip gloss over her lips. When she finishes, she comes up to me and stops.

"Are you sure you are okay with me going out for a little bit?"

"Of course. It's not like we have any plans tonight."

"Yeah, okay. I'm hoping to get some you know, a little winter fling."

I laugh. That's all I can do. We came here to leave the world behind. I guess a one-night stand is one way to do that.

I point to the door. "Go on now. Don't keep the man waiting."

Marina smiles, and I swear I see red creeping on her cheeks. "Do you want me to bring you back anything? Should I be back for dinner?"

"No, I'll eventually head down and see what there is. Worse case, I can order something to be delivered."

"All right, girl, if you change your mind, shoot me a text."

I give her one final salute before she heads out. The second the door clicks, I hear it.

The silence.

Standing, I walk up to the window. The snow is coming down now. Well, here is to hoping I find something to eat inside the ski resort because I really don't want to venture out while it's snowing. Sounds lame, but I prefer the snow on the ground, not raining down over me.

I sigh as I grab my room card, phone, and wallet. This is our first time staying at Gravity Ski Hill, and I really have no idea what they have in terms of places to grab food.

When I hit the lobby, the first place I pass is the

lounge. There, nestled at the end of the bar, is my best friend and the dark-haired hottie. If I didn't know them, I would assume they were lovers. Lovers that look like they are madly in love.

Ugh. Leave it to Marina to find romance while on a girls trip.

I pass by a gift shop before I spot a little cafe, market type of place. Since I'm not certain what I want, I decide to check it out. One side has snacks and drinks. The other side has what looks like made to order sandwiches, wraps, and salads. A grilled chicken wrap with avocado actually sounds good, but so does a chicken Cesar salad.

Decisions, decisions.

Since it is still early, I hold off on ordering and head back over to the other side to grab myself water and a wild berry seltzer. I also grab a Reese's Cup for dessert. I know, it's the perfect combo.

Only one person is working the check out and the line is long. Great.

I'm mindlessly reading the ingredients on the back of my candy when suddenly someone bumps into me. Both my water and my Reese Cup fall from my hands.

"Shit! I am so sorry!" a voice calls out. A male's voice.

Just as I try to reach down while trying to process what just happened, that same person leans forward and our heads collide. Instantly I grab my head at the same time this person steps forward, crushing my Reese's Cups.

"Oh my god! Do you—" I stop short when I take in the guy standing in front of me. The gorgeous guy standing in front of me. Blonde shaggy hair. Baby blue eyes. He has to be at least six-two.

"I am so damn sorry." He runs a hand through his hair

"I... um... it is okay."

"How is your head?" He reaches out and moves my hand that is still holding my head. "Shit, we should get some ice on that."

I shrug. "I have this." I hold up my seltzer and lean it against the tender spot.

"Yeah, I guess alcohol works."

Great. Now I feel stupid. Not sure what else to do or even say, I look down and my crushed candy.

"Shit. I am really sorry, let me get you another."

"I can do that," I say, but he is already gone.

He returns less than a minute later with not one but two Reese Cups. I raise an eyebrow in question.

"I saw yours and now I want one."

"Oh."

"Hey." He turns and smiles back at me. God, this is so damn awkward.

"Yeah?"

"I'm really sorry."

"It's fine. I'll be okay."

"Are you here with someone?"

"What?"

"Are you staying here with someone? You know, boyfriend, family?"

"Girls trip."

"Why are you alone?"

"She found a date for the night." I roll my eyes and then stop and realize I am talking to a stranger.

Why the hell am I telling a stranger this shit? I have seen plenty of documentaries. This is how women disappear and end up dead.

"I was supposed to be out here with my girl-friend. I had plans to propose. That was until she left me last week."

"Wow, um… I'm sorry."

"Don't be. In hindsight, I dodged a bullet."

"Yeah," I reply because what else does one say.

The line moves, and it's his turn at the register. I breathe in a sigh of relief. This entire situation has been strange.

He glances back with what can only be described as the perfect smile plastered on his face.

Once I'm done paying, I head over to the condi-ment station to grab a couple of napkins. When I walk out, the guy is standing just outside of the market.

"We meet again," I say as I walk past him. He is quick and keeps pace with me.

"I was, um, thinking if you didn't have plans since, you know, your friend is out on a date that maybe we could grab dinner."

"Dinner with a stranger, no thanks."

"I know, it sounds crazy. Just hear me out first."

I stop and face him. "Fine, let's hear it. Tell me why going to dinner with a complete stranger would be a great idea."

"For starters, I'm alone, and you're alone tonight. I thought instead of eating dinner alone, we could grab dinner together."

"I am totally fine eating by myself."

"Come on, no one likes eating alone."

I chew my lip. He is right, dammit.

"What's your name?" I ask. If I am going to commit to some wild idea, I should at least look the guy up.

"Dane."

"Do you have a last name, Dane?"

"It's Patterson. Are you going to tell me your name?"

"Callia."

"Do you have a last name, Callia?"

"I do, but you aren't getting it."

"Fair enough. Are you always so feisty?" he asks with amusement in his blue eyes.

"Yes."

He nods. "Noted. So, what do you say? Dinner?"

I am debating on what to do when we walk past the lounge. I stop and glance in. Marina and Leon are still sitting there. He casually tucks a stray piece of hair behind her ear. Ugh. See, they could be a couple in some romance movie.

"Is that your friend?"

Shit. Dane. I forgot about him.

"You're still here."

"Uh, I was walking next to you." He nods

toward Marina. "I don't think your friend is going to be returning anytime soon."

I shake my head and start walking again.

"Come on, Callia, go to dinner with me. Instead of us sulking alone, we can pretend for a little bit."

"I don't know," I say when I reach the elevator. I refuse to punch a button. I don't want him knowing what floor I'm staying on.

"Eight pm. Gravity Divine."

"I'll think about it."

Dane nods and hits the button for floor ten. The doors to the elevator open and he steps in. He waves goodbye as the door shuts.

I'm left standing there alone. To eat dinner with him or eat dinner alone.

Decisions, decisions.

three

· · ·

Plopping down on the hotel bed, I open my drink. I take a long sip before unlocking my phone. I open Instagram and search Dane Patterson.

Like I suspected, loads of accounts with the same name come up. I waste time scrolling until I spot a familiar face. I click the name and get to snooping.

Dane Patterson is a twenty-something adventure seeker. So his bio says.

I pop a chocolate peanut butter cup in my mouth and check out every single one of his photos. While I don't know exactly where he resides, I do know that many of his pictures are along the coast-line. He loves to surf, and man, has his skin been kissed by the sun.

I pause when I click on a photo of him and a female. This must be the girlfriend. Her arms are wrapped around his neck. She smiles for the camera, meanwhile Dane's eyes are on her. He looks happy and in love. Sadly their relationship is no more.

I sigh and think about my own relationship woes. Juan and I spent four and a half years together. I was faithful the entire time. He, on the other hand, was not. It's been six months and yes, I am still salty.

After browsing a little bit more, I start to feel like Dane from the market is a little less like a stranger. The question still remains, do I actually go to dinner with him? Is he going to want more? The restaurant is a public setting and it's not like he gave me creeper vibes. It's just dinner. What was it he said? Something about pretending.

You know what? Pretending sounds fun right about now.

Live a little, I tell myself.

After popping the second Reese's Cup in my mouth, I head for the bathroom to freshen up. I have no desire for anything else other than dinner, yet here I am shaving my legs.

Thankfully, I packed something decent to wear to this fake dinner. I slide into a black long-sleeve jumpsuit. It's satin. Iridescent beading lines the plunging neckline. It is sexy, yet classy at the same time. Grabbing my favorite ColourPop palette, I walk back into the bathroom. My black eyes stare back at me as I apply a smokey gray look. I add a swipe of silver glitter for good measure. Once satisfied, I spray a little setting spray.

I glance at my phone to check on the time. I still

have time. My hair is the last thing that needs done. Running a brush through my dark strands has always calmed me. I hope it will now because I would be lying if I said I wasn't nervous.

I laugh. This is wild. Crazy even. Yet, here I am dressed and ready to go on this so called date.

I walk past the hotel mirror before I head out. I stop to look at myself one last time.

My father is from Mexico. My mother, Florida. She is fair skinned, light brown hair, and green eyes. Her genetics never stood a chance against my father's. I smile. I am a female version of him. His twin.

When I see the neon light reading Gravity Divine ahead, my heart rate picks up. Not sure why, it is just dinner.

With a hot guy that I don't know.

"Callia." His husky voice makes me pause before I reach the podium. I turn to find him standing just a few feet away. And fuck me if he doesn't ooze sex.

I smile. "Dane."

His blue eyes light up at my words. His blonde hair is disheveled as if he just came in from the storm. Like me, he changed his clothes. The gray and blue flannel that he is wearing compliment his eyes.

He looks good.

"You came."

"I did."

He nods, taking two long strides to reach me. He holds an arm out for me to take, but I hesitate.

"It's fine. We're pretending, remember."

Oh yeah.

I link my hand through his and allow him to take the lead. He nods to the hostess, but doesn't say a word as we walk past. That's odd.

"Um, are you just going to seat us yourself?" I ask as we continue making our way through the restaurant.

"Yes and no," is all he says.

Red flags go up and I slow my stride. Dane senses this so he stops, turning to face me. He wears a sinister smile, yet there is humor in his eyes.

"Relax, Callia. My family owns this resort. I called ahead for a reservation."

Oh wow! I was not expecting that response. Not one bit. He must see the shock on my face because he chuckles lightly.

"Come on."

I nod, allowing him to lead us to a table that has a window view, and not just any view. This view of Breckenridge is absolutely breathtaking.

Dane holds the seat out for me like a gentleman. I take it and then look back out the window. Snow falls over the already snow-covered mountains.

"Beautiful, isn't it?"

"Yes, it really is."

I have to force my eyes away from the view. "Your family really owns this resort?"

"Yeah." He shrugs. "It is not a big deal though."

No big deal? Gravity Ski Hill isn't just any resort. It's a high-end ski resort. I know what Marina and I are paying to stay here. It's a miracle we didn't have to sell our kidneys on the black market.

"I see that look on your face."

I scoff. "What look?"

"The one where you are in shock. I've seen it many times."

"Uh, do you bring women here often?"

Dane laughs. "No. You are actually the first woman I have ever brought to dinner here."

"What about your ex-girlfriend? Surely you have brought her here?"

He must be lying, trying to woo me or some bullshit. I ain't buying it though.

"Well, I had plans to take her to dinner here, but no. She has never been out here."

His voice almost sounds sad. I want to feel bad, except I don't know this guy enough to feel any sort of way.

"Then how have you seen the shocked expression many times?"

"My friends come out often. People I've taught, they all look at me the same."

"Oh."

The waitress, a beautiful woman with curly brown hair and eyes that match, takes our drink orders. Dane also orders a tuna poke to start. I sure hope he doesn't plan to share that with me. He'll be in for quite the shock when I do not touch it.

Once the waitress leaves, Dane speaks. "I hope you don't mind that I ordered us an appetizer."

I laugh. "Not at all."

"What's so funny?"

How do I put this nicely, without hurting his feelings? "I, um, do not eat seafood."

"No seafood? As in, none, no shellfish? Not any kind of fish?"

I shake my head.

Dane's face morphs, and I instantly feel horrible. Without thinking I spit out the first thing that comes to mind.

"It's not a big deal. Isn't that what you said?"

"It is, I can order something else." His eyes scan the room for the waitress.

I reach across the table and place my hand on his. His baby blues shoot to our hands briefly before they find mine. "Tell me something, Dane, did you order the tuna because you like it or did you order it for me?"

"Both," he replies without hesitation.

"Then don't change the appetizer. You should still get it and enjoy it."

He nods. "Okay, only if you're sure."

"Totally sure. In fact I'll be disappointed if you cancel it."

A crooked smile appears on his lips. I like it. It suits him.

It is almost comical how this is playing out so far. So much for pretending. His family owns this place, and I just told him I do not eat creatures from the sea. We sure are off to an honest start.

four

. . .

We stare at each other. Actually, I am combing over each and every one of his facial features. Light stubble covers his strong jaw line. He is quite the perfect specimen.

I wonder if he is a good kisser.

I mean I should at least have a little fun right? Marina is out after all.

Someone clears their throat, and my thoughts snap back to the present.

The pretty waitress is back with our drinks. I lift my hand to take my drink and realize it was still on top of Dane's.

He never pulled away.

I didn't either though.

"You know, you two are such an adorable couple."

She thinks we're a couple. Shit.

I open my mouth to tell her we are just friends, but Dane reaches and grabs my hand. There's a spark of excitement in his eyes. "You think so?" he asks, shocking me further.

I arch an eyebrow at him, what is he up to?

"Oh yes, it is obvious that you two are smitten with each other. It's written all over your faces. There is this blissful bubble over your table."

Well, if I wasn't blushing before, I sure as shit am now. This poor woman thinks two strangers are dating.

Someone should tell her.

"Dane and I—"

"Are taking things slow. We don't like to put a label on us," Dane cuts me off. Meanwhile, I stare at the man in complete shock.

"That is smart. Labels can sometimes ruin a good thing and you two got a good thing."

"I agree," he states.

Unable to speak for fear of screwing up Dane's little game with the waitress, I reach for my glass of wine and just nod.

"Are you two ready to order or would you like more time?"

"I'm ready. Callia?"

The way Dane says my name, it rolls off his tongue perfectly. I have never thought my name could sound sexy, but this stranger just went and did it. I squeeze my thighs and try to focus on the menu.

"Yes, I know what I want."

"Perfect, ladies first."

"I'm going to go with the mushroom risotto."

"That comes with a Gravity salad. Oil and vinegar okay?"

"Yes, that's fine, thank you."

"And for you?"

"Gravity short ribs, with roasted asparagus."

"Great, I'll get these in."

"Thanks," Dane replies.

The entire time, his eyes never leave mine. It makes me feel some kind of way. I'd say it is a mixture of excitement and feeling fully alive.

"You didn't want to play along?" he asks, his voice serious.

I can't help but shake my head while laughing at him. "It's not that, I just wasn't expecting it."

"Yeah, but did you hear her? What she said about us? We look good together." Dane winks as he takes a sip of his drink. Is that water he has in his glass?

"Are you drinking water?"

He looks down at his glass and then back to me. "Yeah, I don't drink much, and sugary drinks aren't healthy."

"I see."

"You think I'm lame, don't you?"

"Not at all. I'm kind of impressed. Usually, jocks are all about getting drunk to look cool."

"Who said I'm a jock?" He acts offended as he places a hand on his chest.

I can't tell him I was snooping Insta. Nope, no way. Lie, pretend. Ugh, I am going to need more wine.

"No one said you were, I was just assuming."

"That hurt."

"Are you a jock?"

"No way. I mean, I am athletic and active. A jock, no."

"Is that so?"

I smirk at his failed attempt to look crushed. "That is the most pitiful face I think I have ever seen."

The waitress comes back with his sushi and my salad. I'm thankful for that because now he won't feel guilty eating it in front of me.

"Beautiful, isn't it?" He nods to the window.

"Yes."

"Just like you."

My eyes leave the window and focus on those blue eyes. He gives nothing anyway. I can't tell if his words hold truth or if he's pretending.

The further into this dinner, the more the two seem to blend.

And I might just be okay with that.

five

. . .

"Want to see something cool?" Dane asks as we exit the restaurant.

"Uh, sure. Let me just check in with Marina real quick."

He nods and steps away as if to give me privacy. If only he lived back home in Florida. The guys there do not seem to understand the term personal space. At least not the guys that I've dated anyway.

I pull up Marina's number on my phone and hit the call button. It barely rings two times.

"Hey, babe!" my friend answers cheerfully, "What's up?"

"Hey, I was just checking in. Everything good on your end?"

"Oh yeah!" she practically gushes. I bet her cheeks are beet red too.

"That's good. Hey, listen, I am going out for a bit."

"Wait! With who, because I know you aren't going anywhere alone."

She's right. I wouldn't just go to a bar, club, or any other people-ly place alone.

"I, uh, met someone while in the market." I try to speak quietly. Dane may have stepped away, but that doesn't mean he can't eavesdrop.

"What do you mean a someone?"

"His name is Dane. We thought it would be fun to go on a fake date."

"Callia, are you feeling okay? This is so out of character of you."

"I know."

"Tell me all the things!"

"Marina, chill." I try to whisper. "It is fine. I am fine. I will tell you everything later."

I end the call and walk up to my fake dinner date. "So you wanted to show me something?"

"I do. All good with your friend?"

"Yes."

We get on an elevator, and Dane swipes with room card over the keypad. Weird, I don't have to do that to get to my floor. No numbers light up either, yet I can tell we are going up.

The doors open and I follow him out. We start to walk down a corridor. It's quiet and the only people I have passed are employees. They smile as they continue on their way.

Surely if Dane was going to harm me, he wouldn't bring me out where employees could see us, right?

We come up to a door and once again, he pulls out his room card. Before he puts it against the reader on the door, he turns to me. "Um." He runs a hand through his hair. He is nervous and that makes me slightly nervous in return.

"You can choose to leave at any time. Just say the word."

What the fuck? I raise an eyebrow. "Should I be scared of what is behind that door?"

"No, nothing scary. However, you should know, it is my room. The cool thing I want to show you is in there."

"Do you have anything that can harm me?" I don't know why I ask, I just do.

"No, of course not. Look, you can stand in the doorway if you don't feel comfortable."

"Okay," I say as I pull my phone out. Dane looks down at it and then looks up at me. A crooked smile plays at his lips.

"I am no dummy."

"I know."

Without another word, he taps the card, and a green light appears. He opens the door and walks in. The lights are on, but he walks up to the light switch anyway.

"Now don't freak out, just wait and let your eyes adjust."

I am starting to think Mr. Adventurer has lost his damn mind as the room goes dark.

I do what he says. I allow my eyes to adjust to

the darkness; my foot still has the door propped, leaving my stance awkward.

As my eyes fully adjust, I see the glow coming from the huge glass window. The curtains are tied back. Dane is already standing in front of it.

Curiosity gets the best of me. I take a few steps in. The sky is dark, that much I can tell. So where is the glow coming from?

I'm about two feet behind Dane, yet I still can't tell.

"I did not bring you here to harm you, Callia. Come and enjoy this with me."

Deciding his words hold truth, I walk and stand next to him. My eyes shoot downward.

"Wow," it is the first word that comes to mind.

"Right?"

Down below is the town. Houses are lit up, chimneys smoking. There is a fully lit Christmas tree in what appears to be the town's center. A bright star sits proudly at the top. It looks like a real-life Michael Kincaid village. It is beautiful.

"I just wanted to share this with someone and since you agreed to our date, I knew I wanted that someone to be you."

"Thank you for sharing this with me."

I can feel his eyes on me, however, I am too mesmerized to look at him.

I am not sure how much time passes. I allow myself to get lost in the snowy scene below. Tonight has been good. I went on a random date with a stranger and really enjoyed myself. Dane is good looking. Dinner was nice. He took care of the bill even after I asked to cover my half. He's been a total gentleman.

"Callia." Dane's voice snaps me out of my head. "You okay?" I hear the concern in his voice.

"Yeah, I was just enjoying the view. Taking it all in."

"I told you it was cool."

Dane comes to stand a little closer to me.

"You're a man of your word it would seem." I give him a wink as the butterflies start to take flight. The way he looks at me, smiles at me. I like it. I watch as Dane's eyes drift to my lips before meeting my eyes.

"Can I kiss you?"

Well, I was not expecting those words to come out of his mouth. I hardly know this man, but what the hell, why not?

"That depends, are you a good kisser?"

He smirks at my words and closes the distance between us. He reaches up and tucks a loose strand of my hair behind my ear.

"There is only one way to find out."

And then his lips land on mine.

Dane kisses me slowly, testing the waters. I, on the other hand, deepen the kiss. I run my hands though his hair. Goodness knows my love life has been slacking.

Dane is a good kisser. He's gentle, yet hard at all the right moments.

My hands leave his hair and reach for his shirt.

He lets me lift it just enough to slide my hands under. I can confirm, his pictures match real life.

My fingers can't help but trace the lines that he has worked hard to define. He is the one to break out kiss. I stare at his lips. Lips that were just on mine.

"So, am I a good kisser?"

"You are."

He nods with that crooked smile of his.

"Now what?" I ask because, if I am being honest, between the alcohol that is still flowing and the fact that we just kissed, I have needs. Needs that he just broke the seal on and there is no way I can return to my hotel room without getting off.

Call me what you will, I don't care. I've been called plenty of things.

Dane swallows. "I, um, I have never done anything like this. The whole fake date, bringing you up here, I was just winging it."

"Then let's just go with it. Let's keep winging it."

Man, I sure sound confident. Either that or I sound like some sort of hussy. It sounds wild. Regardless, I am on vacation, and I deserve to have a good time.

"Let's wing it," Dane responds.

I lean in and kiss him. This time I pull up his shirt and he allows me to remove it.

Winging it. Sounds like the perfect idea.

six

. . .

The second his shirt is over his head, his calloused hands are on me. The way his fingers glide against my skin. I like it. Like really like it. Strangely, this all feels right.

I reach for the button on his jeans only for him to pull back, just out of my reach.

"You gotta catch up." Dane winks as he eyes my chest.

"You're right."

Without a second thought, I pull my jumpsuit top down to my waist. I don't stop there. I unfasten my hot pink bra and let it drop to the ground. Dane's eyes are solely trained on my bare breasts. The cool air causes them to harden right away.

This time when I reach for his jeans, he doesn't pull away. As soon as I have them unbuttoned, his hands touch me. Kneading both breasts before his fingers gently start pinching my nipples. I throw my head back as pleasure starts to flow through my veins.

Dane leans into my breasts, his hot breath sending chills all over me. At first, it's just a swipe of his tongue against my nipple. A tease. The teasing is quickly replaced with sucking, nipping.

I'm frantic as I work to remove his boxer briefs. His erection springs free, and I grip it. He's veiny, thick. No hair, which does not surprise me. His chest was smooth as could be, same with his arms. I imagine his legs will be void of any hair too.

Dane lets go of my nipple to focus on removing the rest of my clothes. I almost help him. Almost. Instead, I take the time to take him in.

To take him in, all his naked glory.

He is athletic, no doubt about that. Broad shoulders, toned in all the right places. Muscular calves and just like I suspected, zero hair on his legs.

"Like what you see?" Dane's sexy voice distracts me from eye-fucking him.

I throw a hand on my hip and realize that not only are my pants down around my ankles, but so are the leggings that I wore under. I must have been too busy checking him out to realize he got them off. I glance up and smirk.

"As a matter of fact, I do like what I see. You should do something about it."

His eyes rake over every inch of my body. He leans in and grips me behind my thighs. He lifts me up and I wrap my legs around him. As he walks with me to his bed, I know without a doubt, that he can feel how wet I am. Just the thought should have me feeling embarrassed, yet it doesn't. It does the complete opposite. I feel confident and one hundred percent comfortable in this man's arms.

Have I gone mad?

I'm starting to think I have.

As soon as he lays me down on his bed, he leans up on his arms.

"You are breathtaking."

"Thank you." My words come out quiet. For all I know he could just be throwing me a line. Not that I care, I am consenting to this after all.

"I mean it. I know we're just winging it, but you are breathtaking."

I hear the sincerity in his words, I do. But right now, I just want to get railed. He must read my mind because his hand slides up my thigh between my legs. If he didn't feel how wet I was as he carried me, he sure does now. He sinks a finger into me, pumping a few times before he pulls it out. He lifts it to his lips before sliding it into his mouth where he proceeds to suck my juices off of it.

It is the hottest fucking thing, I swear.

Dane moans as he slides his finger from his mouth. His other hand is wrapped firmly around his cock.

This has to be one of the most erotic experiences of my life. In a hotel room with a stranger. Naked on the bed with him doing such intimate things. I replay what he just did over in my head. It has me so hot that without realizing it, my hand has snaked down my stomach. Before I can stop myself, I begin teasing my clit. Bolts of electricity send shocks throughout my body. My eyes start to drift close while I continue touching myself in front of Dane.

"Fuck," he says.

My eyes blink open. His hand is still firmly on his cock. He is slowly stroking it. How did we get here? Hours earlier we agreed to be each other's fake dinner date and now we are masturbating in front of each other.

I shake my head to keep from laughing. This is wild.

Crazy.

Yet, I am enjoying every second of it. Each time I flick, I am one second closer to coming apart. One second closer to Dane fucking me.

Just as I feel myself begin to tremble, Dane reaches out and grabs my hand, stopping me. I raise an eyebrow at him.

"I should be the one who makes you come." He gives me a quick wink before grabbing my thighs to pull me closer to the edge of the bed.

Who is this man and where has he been? Saying such a thing is enough to make a girl combust. Dane does not give me time to dwell on such dirty thoughts because his tongue hits my clit.

He entire mouth is on my most sensitive parts, doing unspeakable things. The sensation from his tongue alone makes my back arch while I moan out loud.

Dane inserts a finger into me while he continues

pleasuring me with his tongue. It drives me straight over the edge. Gripping the white sheets, I scream out as my orgasm rips through me. I can see stars for days.

He does not let up. His tongue keeps swirling around my swollen clit. My hands fist his hair to attempt to pull him up. It works, kind of.

"Come one more time for me," Dane says with his voice laced with lust. How does one say no to that?

"Okay, okay. And then you promise to fuck me?"

He smirks. "Promise."

Sighing dreamily, I lay back as his mouth lands back on me. He wastes zero time.

This time my orgasm comes on faster, stronger. My legs shake uncontrollably as I scream out. What, I don't even know or care.

By the time I open my eyes, Dane is sliding on a condom. Smart man. I will give him that. I sit up on my elbows in anticipation of what is next.

Dane comes to hover over me. He lines his cock up at my entrance. I can't resist the urge to grind into him.

"Impatient, are we?" He gives me a sexy grin as he slowly sinks into me, stretching me. I knew he was thick just by the sight of him, but damn. He feels massive.

He finally starts to move his hips a little faster. Harder.

"Fuck," I pant as he picks up the pace.

Dane leans back, sliding out of me. Before I can object or question, he grabs my hips, flipping me on my stomach. He pulls my hips up and drives his cock straight back into my pussy.

He fucks me hard. And he doesn't stop.

The sound of our skin connecting echoes throughout the hotel room. I can feel yet another orgasm building. Each time he thrusts into me, it intensifies.

With my face in the sheets to muffle my screams and moans, I come again, rocking into Dane while he chases his own orgasm.

And when he comes, he comes hard.

When it is over, my knees give out. Dane collapses on top of me for a split second before rolling to his side. He wipes my sweaty hair from my face.

"Holy shit."

Holy shit is right. All I do is nod while smiling in return. My unplanned mission is complete. I told myself I wanted to get railed and Dane came through. There's an ache between my legs and I know I will feel it tomorrow. I smile at the thought.

"Now what?" Dane asks, popping my magical little bubble.

That is a good question. Now what?

seven

. . .

Grabbing my clothes, I head for the bathroom to clean myself up. Dane does not stop me, nor does he say a single word.

For that I am thankful.

Now what? That's the magical question that keeps replaying in my head. Do I stay? Do I go?

I should go, right? Like thanks for dinner and a good time.

What would Marina do? There is a chance she would probably stay the night with the guy and cook him breakfast in the morning. On the other hand, she would leave after without so much as a word.

I silently groan while washing my hands. I splash a little water on my face in an attempt to help me cool my thoughts.

It does very little to help.

I decide that I'll go back to my room. It's my first night here and I do not need to stay the night in some stranger's bed. I may have let him fuck me in it, but sleeping in it too, no, not a wise idea.

When I walk out, Dane is sitting on the edge of the bed with his head in his hands.

"Hey." I try to sound casual as I grab my small purse off the long dresser that doubles as a little wet bar. A flat screen is positioned above it.

Dane looks up, tilts his head slightly. "What are you doing?"

"I'm going to head out." I shrug my shoulders like it's no biggie.

"You are just going to leave? Just like that?"

Dane seems wounded at my words. He stands immediately.

"Uh, It was fun playing pretend for the evening."

"Playing?" He turns and points at the bed. "You thought that was pretending?"

"Well, yeah?" I mean what do I even say? This is already awkward enough for me.

"Callia, I just had my mouth on your pussy and you still thought I was pretending? I thought we were past that when we said we would just see what happens." Hurt laces his words. It's written all over his face.

I am still going to leave even though I feel bad.

"It is not that big of a deal. Just sex."

His face scrunches at my words for a split second before he regains composure. He gets up and walks to the hotel door. Once open, he turns my way, but does not make eye contact with me.

So much for not making this weird.

I quietly walk in Dane's direction. Once I am past him and in the narrow hallway, he speaks up.

"You know, I had a really nice time tonight. Was going to ask if you wanted to see me again, but I see your mind is already made up."

I open my mouth to speak, but Dane continues.

"It's okay, really. We were just pretending, remember?" His eyes meet mine for a split second before looking past me.

I nod my head once in shame. Why I suddenly feel it, I am not sure.

"Have a good night, Callia." He shuts the door, leaving me in the hallway of The Gravity Ski Hill resort.

I did a complete walk a shame the entire way to the elevator. I am sensitive between my legs. A reminder of what I did less than an hour ago. Should I have stayed?

I push the round number four on the keypad and wait. As soon as the doors close, I breathe a sigh of relief. That was so damn weird. I mean the night started off amazing and Dane was every bit of a sweetheart. He was respectful and never made me feel forced into anything that we did.

It is me.

I'm the asshole.

I probably could have gone about that a little better. In my defense, I do not have one-night stands. Hell, it has been a very long time since I have had a random hookup.

The elevator comes to a halt and the bell dings, letting me know I am one step closer to my hotel room. I cannot wait to get to my room to wash the night away.

What I am not expecting when the doors slide open is to see my best friend making out with the tall, dark, and handsome man that she ran off with earlier.

I clear my throat. They both take a sudden step away from each other.

They both speak at the same time.

"Excuse us."

"Oh hey, Callia!" Marina's all bright and cheery. "We were just going. . ." She pauses, not finishing her sentence.

It is then that I notice a bag on his shoulder. Leon, is it? Hell, I can't remember. My mind is a jumbled mess.

"How was your date? The fake date?"

It takes everything for me to not cringe at her words. "It was good, fun."

Marina's eyes turn to slits as she assesses me. I know she is analyzing those four words. She will pick me apart piece by piece later. I can already feel it.

"Hmm..." she says while eyeing me up and down.

I wonder if she can smell the sex on me, because I can.

"We were going to go to Leon's room for a little bit, but if you need me, I can stay back."

"No." I laugh, but it's fake and forced. "You two go on. I'm tired, probably just going to go to bed."

Marina squints her eyes tighter. So close that they might as well be closed. I know what she is doing. She is silently telling me that we WILL be discussing this. She WILL not let it go.

I take a step in the direction of our room and stop. This time it's Leon who clears his throat.

"You are welcome to join us."

WOW!

Just when I thought this night couldn't get any more awkward, it does.

eight

· · ·

"Come on, Mariana! Let's go skiing." I nudge her sleepy form.

She groans as she rolls away from me. I nudge her with a little more force this time. "We only have three more days here. No time to waste."

That does the trick. Marina huffs but sits up and rubs her eyes. Last night she did not come back after I ran into her. I had a suspicion when I saw the bag on her shoulder. She returned early this morning. Six am early.

"What time is it?"

"It's nearly noon. We can grab something quick from the cafe before heading out."

"Fine."

I clap my hands in excitement. I need this. I need to get out of this room and away from this hotel for a bit. My mind keeps drifting back to blonde hair and blue eyes. I need to change that. Last thing I need is for me to return from this vacation and only have Dane to think about.

Ha! Who am I kidding? I will think of Dane when I return home. There is no doubt.

Thirty minutes later, Marina finally emerges from the bathroom, fully dressed and ready to go. I grab my beanie and put it on. My dark hair is in a loose braid. It makes no sense to do much else to it. It's not like I have to impress anyone. Marina, on the other hand, has make-up on and her hair pulled back into some fancy bun.

As soon as the door clicks shut Marina asks the question I had been hoping she would not.

"So, what happened last night?"

"Nothing. We went to dinner and that was it."

Her hand shoots out hitting the elevator button before I can. "Don't lie. You are not one to run off with a stranger. You looked flushed when I saw you. Something happened."

"Fine, we went to dinner and had sex. I ran out after."

"You what?!" she squeals.

I'm thankful that we're alone because I know she is going to grill me.

"Callia! You had a one-night stand? With a stranger? Did you use protection?"

"Yes, God, yes. Do you think I'm dumb?"

"You did something reckless. Normal for me maybe, but not you. No, this is so not like you. Was he at least hot?"

"Oh, he was hot. So damn hot," I state as the elevator comes to a stop.

"What did he look like?"

The doors open and there stands Dane. We went up? We must not have paid attention to the arrow when we stepped into the elevator. He looks equally shocked to see me. The doors begin to shut. He throws his hand out before finally stepping in.

"Callia." Dane nods, then turns his back to me.

I stand there with my mouth wide open. I know I should probably say something, yet no words come.

I can feel Marina staring at me, but I cannot bring myself to look at her. She will read me like an open book.

Hell, she already is.

"Is that him? The guy you screwed last night?" Marina whispers.

Dane stands taller and I know without a doubt that he heard her. I nudge Marina to get her to keep quiet.

"Oh, my lord! It is him. Isn't it?"

I shake my head, silently pleading for her to just shut up. The elevator comes to a stop and just as the doors open, Dane slams his palm over the button that closes the door. The elevator starts to descend.

"Yes, I'm the guy Callia fucked last night." He doesn't turn to look at us. "She let me fuck her, and then she took off."

My best friend gasps, and I cringe at the same

time. He made that sound so horrible. So damn horrible.

Now I know I should speak up and at least try to explain myself. Instead, I stand there covering my face like a coward.

"Callia!" Marina says, "Was he bad in bed? This is so not like you."

My head snaps up. "What? No. That's not what. . . can we just not talk about this?"

We ride in a strange silence the rest of the way down. As soon as we step into the lobby, Dane turns and looks at me before addressing Marina.

"If you figure out why she ran off, let me know because I was hoping to get to know her better."

She nods.

He turns and disappears in the sea of people coming in and out of the lobby.

Marina gives me a smile as she loops her hand through my arm. "You can tell me all about it on the ski lift."

Great. Just great.

nine

. . .

I am in a good mood by the time we return from skiing. It was a complete shit show, yet it was so much fun. Another thing to add to the list of things I cannot do.

I am yanking off my gloves as we walk into the lobby.

"Wanna grab a hot chocolate?" I ask.

"Duh!" Marina laughs.

We grab out hot chocolates and head up to the cashier. Marina nudges me. I look at her and she nods her head behind me. I turn to see Dane at the deli counter. I turn back and give Marina a pointed look. "What?"

"You should at least explain to him. Tell him about Juan and how you are a bit rusty."

She's right.

I hate it, yet she is right.

We walk out of the cafe. I pause nodding, "Fine, meet you back in the room?"

"Uh, actually, would you be okay if I caught up with Leon for a little while?"

"Yeah, go. I need some time to clear my head."

"Clear your head from what?"

Dane's sultry voice comes from behind. Marina smiles at him and waves. She turns and leaves quickly.

I'm glad one of us can escape.

Taking a sip of my drink, I turn to face Dane. Might as well own my shit.

"I'm sorry about last night. I am not very good at this sort of thing."

"You took off like I did something wrong."

"No, no, Dane." I shake my head. "You did nothing wrong. You were a gentleman and amazing and I just, I did not know what to do next. Clearly, I am not good at having a fling or pretending to be whatever." I realize I am word vomiting. I can't help it. I hold my cup close to my mouth, ready to take a sip when Dane comes in close. He pushes my hand down gently.

"I thought we moved past that pretending game when I brought you into my bed."

Well, when he says it like that.

It gives me goosebumps. I remember the way his hands roamed my body. The way he took control.

"Callia."

His lips are now inches from mine. If I were to lean forward a centimeter, our lips would touch and it would be game over.

"Dane, it's not like this can really go anywhere."

"You don't know that," he states firmly.

"I do."

Why am I fighting this? It is obvious, he wants me. I want him. The thing is we live two very different lives.

And I do not want to get hurt. Again.

"This is fun and while I do enjoy being with you, I'm not ready to put myself out there to be hurt again."

"Who said I was going to hurt you?"

"No one," I answer honestly.

Dane closes the gap between us. He kisses me softly before pulling back slightly.

"Why can't we just enjoy each other? We can figure out the rest as we go. Like last night. Take it as it comes."

He makes it sound so simple.

"Dane! There you are!!" a very excited voice yells from the distance.

A female's voice.

Dane freezes for a few seconds, then steps away from me. He looks around until he spots whoever the voice belongs to.

A petite blonde rushes up and throws herself at Dane, wrapping her arms around his neck. She plants a long kiss on his lips.

My lips were just in that exact same spot. Not even five minutes ago. Jealousy and anger suddenly flow through my veins. Dane is real slick thinking he could just feed me lines.

I consider myself a friendly person, however, I already dislike this fake looking chick. Her voice is squeaky. It annoys me. Not as much as Dane has me annoyed, but pretty damn close.

Her tits are clearly bought along with her blonde curls that bounce perfectly each time she moves her head.

I want to front him.

I want to warn her that her man is cheating on her.

I want to tell her that she deserves better.

I deserve better.

I stand there longer than I should and by the time I realize this, Dane has taken a step back and is holding his girl at an arm's length.

"Sasha. Uh, what are you doing here?"

"Oh, you know, I missed you so I figured I would fly out and surprise you. Aren't you surprised to see me?"

"I'm surprised all right."

This Sasha chick laughs. It sounds fake, like she is acting. She reaches out and playfully shoves Dane.

I can't take another minute of their interaction. I slide past them and get a few feet away before Dane calls my name. I stop but I don't look back.

"Callia, wait a minute."

For some reason his words irk me. I turn and hold my hot chocolate up.

"Pretending, remember?" I smirk and walk away, not bothering to give him a chance to explain.

There is no need for him to.
One last fling before the ring or however it goes.
I was just a fill-in.

ten

. . .

I make it back to my hotel room. Dane did not come after me. For that I am glad. I did not want any sort of confrontation. I may be angry and hurt, but I really did not want to cause a scene.

I remind myself that I did nothing wrong. Dane was the one lying. He truly was pretending. It also should not upset me. We were both pretending.

Fuck, I need something stronger than the hot chocolate in my hand. I look in the beverage cooler knowing damn well we only have seltzers. I need more than a girly drink right now. I need tequila. Yes, tequila will work.

Grabbing my room card, I rush out of my room and only freeze when I get to the elevator area. I can't go back down there. There is no way I can risk running into the two of them. I walk back to my room and decide to wait twenty minutes or so. They should be gone by then. Right?

I hesitate as I step out into the lobby. The last

"

thing I need is to run into Dane and his girlfriend. My eyes dart around until I feel confident that they are no longer around.

When I reach the little market, cafe, whatever it is called, I walk past while looking in. It's silly, I know. Yet, I do it anyway.

I do not see him. Or her for that matter. I may have only seen her briefly, but I would be able to pick her out of a damn lineup if given one.

The way her perfect blonde curls fell down her back. Her smile was beaming. She was beautiful.

I sigh, finally walking in. I came down here for one reason and one reason only.

Tequila.

Passing by the candy aisle, I stop and grab not one, but three Reese's Cups. The hell with it. I'll throw myself a pity party. A pity party over some guy I do not even know.

When I reach the alcohol, I scan the shelf looking over my options. There aren't many. Not that I expected there to be, but I don't recognize any of these brands.

"Callia."

I freeze at Dane's voice. My hand is in mid-air, ready to grab a bottle. I let it drop to my side, but don't turn around.

"I was hoping to find you."

"No reason to find me."

"Look, I can explain."

Grabbing a random bottle from the shelf, I finally turn to face him. Damn he looks good wearing that gray beanie. I shake away the thought and focus.

"The only explaining you need to do is to your girlfriend. Explain that you had one last fling before deciding to ask for her hand in marriage."

I shove past Dane, not caring about the hurt that flashes across his face. I'm glad my words hurt him. He deserves it.

"Callia, wait," Dane calls out as he follows me up to the cashier. "Seriously, just give me a minute to explain."

I wave him off while trying to pay attention to the cashier asking to see my ID.

I pull it out and hand it over.

"Would you like this charged to your room?"

"Yes, Room fifty-one twenty-two."'

"You just swipe your room card," Dane says as he stands a little too close to me. His delicious manly scent envelopes me.

Fucking great, now he knows my room number. Maybe he didn't pay attention as I rattled it off.

"Callia, did you hear me? She needs your room card if you are charging it. You know what, I'll pay."

Before I realize what is happening, Dane is swiping his card. The next thing I know the cashier is handing him a receipt.

Shit. Shit. Shit.

Dane reaches for my items before I can. It causes me to shake my head. Why am I so distracted?

Because the man is in my personal space, and he smells good.

As soon as we walk out, Dane heads for a sitting area. The last thing I want to do is sit down to have any sort of conversation with him. I have a date with chocolate and tequila.

I reach for my stuff, but Dane side steps. I glare at him. "Give me my stuff?"

"Talk to me for a minute."

"There is nothing to talk about, Dane. Now give me my stuff."

"Technically, it is my stuff."

He gives me a sly smile. One I want to slap right off of his face. I know I can totally walk back into the market and purchase the items again. Part of me, though, wants to hear what his lame ass has to say.

"Fine, you have one damn minute. Let's get this over with."

Dane sets the tequila down and pulls the beanie off his head.

"Fuck," he says as he runs a hand through his hair. His other hand still holds my Reese's Cups. "What you saw, with Sasha. That is not what it looked like."

I laugh. The audacity of this dude. He must think I'm stupid. I mean I guess I am since I was so close to falling for his smooth words.

"I'm dead ass. We are no longer together. She told me she could not see herself staying with someone like me for the long run. She thinks she needs a man in a suit and tie in order to be happy. That I was a great lover, but Sasha cares about her image and reputation, so she called things off back home."

"That is sort of pathetic," I say truthfully.

He shrugs. "It stung at first."

"Where is home?" I am not sure why I ask. I just do.

"Florida. Tampa area."

He lives in Florida? The same state as me? This is brand new information. Doesn't matter though. We will never be anything.

"And so what, she just jumped on a plane to surprise you at your family's ski resort?"

"She knew I would be here. She ran into a buddy of mine and caught wind that I was going to propose."

Arching an eyebrow, I stare at Dane. I'm not buying it.

"Right, like I am supposed to believe you? It sounds like you are talking out of your ass."

He must be.

"Callia, remember last night at dinner. I told you I had planned to bring my girlfriend out here and that she had never been here. Remember the part where I told you she left me?"

"Oh, I remember. She did, however, come rushing up throwing herself at you and the two of you making out. Right in front of me. Remember that?"

Dane tilts his head up and sighs. You can bet I

am going to call him on his bullshit even if I exaggerate some.

"She flew out here on her own. She knows my family owns this place. What she wasn't prepared for was that no one at the front desk would give her my room information. Finding me standing in the hallway was pure luck on her end. I was in complete shock seeing her. When she kissed me, I was not expecting her to show up and jump into my arms. I would have not allowed it."

There may be some truth to his words. Even still, her being here will put a damper on us. Not that there was an us. I remind myself that we were pretending.

Just pretending.

Does not matter if he is hot.

Does not matter if he is a great kisser.

Does not matter if I enjoyed the things he did to my body.

"Callia," Dane says, snapping me out of my thoughts.

I throw an arm up. "So now what, Dane?" I shake my head. This is all so crazy. "You know what it does not matter. We were just pretending last night. No big deal."

Dane all but drops my peanut butter cups. He steps into my personal space. Real close. His hand grips the back of my neck. The sensation alone causes my skin to prickle with heat.

"I know I said we should just wing it, but do you think I was pretending when my mouth was on your pussy last night?" He swallows thickly. "What about when I sank into your pussy? That I was pretending? That it was all just for fun?"

"I… I don't know, now I'm not sure."

I can't concentrate with him this close. Thoughts of last night swirl in my mind. All I smell is him, and he smells so good. I try not to stare at his lips. It's hard. So damn hard.

"Callia," Dane whispers, sending signals straight to the apex of my thighs.

"Dane—"

I can barely get his name out of my mouth before his lips land on mine.

eleven

. . .

He tastes like a mixture of something salty and something sweet. Something I should not want. Not with his girlfriend, ex-girlfriend close by. For all I know she could be lurking around the corner. That reality sends me reeling backward.

"Really, Dane, let's not make last night a big deal."

Hurt flashes in his eyes once again. He looks taken aback by my words. I want to feel bad, and I almost do, until I remember that he just had a woman jumping into his arms.

Sighing, I force a smile. "Well, this was fun." I turn to go but he grabs my wrist.

"Wait." Dane pauses for a split second. "I had a nice time with you. I meant everything I said. I wasn't just feeding you lines, Callia. There is something about you."

I nod. "Okay."

That is all I give him. Nothing more.

It frustrates him. He is visibly annoyed even though he really has no reason to be.

I cast my eyes down to where his hands are wrapped around my wrist. The heat from his touch does things to me that I'd rather not admit. Like allow him to kiss me once more.

I need him to release me, so I can escape.

I tug a little and he releases me. I give him a sad smile then turn and walk away.

I've just about reached the elevators when I hear Dane call my name.

I stop but do not turn around.

"I need you to believe me."

Ugh. Why does a man as hot as Dane have to say such things?

"Callia, what can I do to prove to you that I wasn't lying about the breakup?"

A few people glance at me as they pass by. Dane is voicing his words to not only me, but to every person that is nearby. That should tell me all I need to know.

He is being truthful.

I turn around.

He starts walking my way. I put my hand up. "Stay right there. I can hear what you have to say from here." That and I am ninety-five percent sure I will cave if he gets all up in my space again.

Damn him for being hot and smelling good.

"Tell me what you want me to do."

I put my hand on my hip in a weak attempt to look confident. "Where did she go?"

"She should be in her room."

"Her room?"

Dane nods. "I refused to let her come up to my room. So I had the front desk book her a room until I can get her back on a plane out of here."

"And then what?"

Dane huffs, while taking a few steps toward me.

.

"She goes home and moves on with her life."

"And what does she have to say about that?"

"She wasn't thrilled to learn that I will not be taking her back." He takes another step forward and then another.

His words come out harsh. Part of me feels bad for the chick. I bet she wasn't expecting him to deny her.

With Dane now only a few steps away, I ask one last question.

"Where do you think this will go?" I point between us.

"I don't know exactly, but I am willing to find out."

"Why?" I ask just before he closes the space between us.

"Because there is something about you. I enjoy being in your presence. Isn't that enough, Callia?"

I shrug my shoulders in response. What else am I supposed to say?

"Take a walk with me?" he asks simply.

"Okay, only for a few though. I have plans." That's a lie, but he doesn't need to know that.

He nods and guides me away from the elevator. We walk in silence until he walks up to the front desk. He hands the front desk clerk my bag of stuff and rattles off my room number.

He remembered it.

He then turns and guides me by my lower back to the entrance. I slow as we step outside.

"Dane?"

"Let me take you to Main Street."

I arch an eyebrow at the man. Has he lost his damn mind? He sure has.

"To where?"

"I want to take you to the downtown area, you know the view from my room. I want to take you there."

He points to a waiting trolley. "Come on." Hope fills his eyes.

"What if I catch hypothermia?"

Dane laughs and shakes his head. "Don't worry, I'll keep you warm."

Dane sure has a way with words. I know I shouldn't entertain this, whatever it is. Yet I step out, deciding to risk my life just this once.

We step off the trolley on Main Street. Dane gives me a minute to take it all in.

The clouds block the sun as snow falls softly around us. Even in the downtown area of Breckenridge, the view that surrounds us is majestic. It is like we are in our little snow globe.

I won't lie, I love it.

But why?

I have no idea.

We walk along the sidewalk until we reach what I assume to be the town center. The Christmas tree is just a few feet away. I stop and just take it all in. The snow, the Christmas lights. The holiday music that comes from somewhere.

"Callia? Did you hear me?" Dane's gentle words bring me back to reality. My eyes find his.

"Uh, no, I did not."

"I like you."

I smirk. "You can't say that. You don't even know me."

He shakes his head. "I like what I do know about you. I like how I feel when I am around you."

Dane pulls me closer. His fingers graze my cheek before tilting my chin toward him. A shiver runs down my spine. I can't tell if it is because of the temperature, or if it's something more.

"I like you," he states again.

"So you've said."

"I also like your sass. You don't seem to put up with shit."

I shrug. "What can I say? I'm an honest person."

"I like that too," he says as he leans in, wrapping a hand around the base of my neck. Before I can protest, his mouth lands on mine.

Dane's gentle at first. Until I open my mouth to invite him in. Then his movements turn almost frantic, like the man cannot get enough of me. Dane's other hand wraps around my back and he pulls me closer.

Our tongues dance while the snow continues to fall. It gets my blood pumping and warmth spreads throughout my entire body. It awakens needs and wants. I try not to grind against him but fail. I want to feel him. Need to feel him. For some reason, I feel eyes on us and would rather this happen in private.

If I were witnessing us, I would like to think we look like a scene from a holiday romance movie.

I am the first to pull back. Dane leans his head against mine. His eyes close. Little breath clouds form from both of us. We are breathing heavily, and it is cold as shit out.

"Can we go back to the resort now? It is too cold for me."

"Only if I can bring you back to my room," he says with his eyes still closed. I don't know why, but I find it hot. His demeanor turns me on more.

"Okay."

Those haunting blue eyes pop open. He wasn't expecting me to agree. He grabs my hand and yanks me back in the direction we just came from. I don't miss his other hand adjusting himself quickly.

I let out a giggle.

I can't believe I'm going to go back to his room for a second time. I must be a gluten for punishment.

Either that or maybe deep down I am hoping for something more.

twelve

. . .

As soon as we step into the elevator, Dane hits the button for his floor and one other button. He does it so fast that I have zero time to process anything. The doors shut before anyone else can step on. I feel bad for the people that were walking up.

That is until Dane walks me back into the corner. He's on me. His hands move under all my layers until he reaches bare skin. He leaves little chills in his wake. When did he have time to remove his gloves I wonder. His mouth finds mine and he kisses me fiercely. I welcome it. I give it right back to him. We can't seem to get enough of each other.

The elevator is still going up as Dane's hand reaches into my bra. Cold fingers graze my nipples, pinching them slightly. His physical touch might be cold, yet here I am burning up. My body is on fire and only Dane can put out the flames. I can't help but grind into him while kissing him.

Can this elevator go any slower, I think to myself

as his hand leaves my breast. He dips it into my waistband, wasting no time finding my clit. Almost instantly, my head falls back.

Little alarm bells start going off in the back of my mind as I feel the elevator start to slow.

However, his finger continues to rub my most sensitive spot, causing me to ignore the warning bells.

Who cares if those doors open?

My eyes drift close and his movements pick up speed. I squirm and grind into him. I need more friction, more something. I can just barely feel his erection, yet it is not enough.

I think I hear a bell, but I am too far gone to care. I'm on the edge of bliss and that is all that matters in this moment. I need to reach that high. Need to reach that level of ecstasy.

Suddenly, Dane's body shifts, and my eyes blink open. He is still strumming my clit like a guitar while his other hand darts out at the keypad. My eyes grow wide as the elevator doors shut and we begin to move again.

Someone could have seen us! Maybe they did! That thought alone excites me. Knowing we were almost caught. The two of us doing something private in public. Dane's fingers move at just the right speed, sending me crashing into that pool of ecstasy. The one I was craving, chasing.

Moans escape my lips as I come apart. He places kisses right below my ear.

"That's right, come all over my fingers."

Hell, how does he make that sound so hot?

All too quickly though, the high begins to leave my body. It leaves me panting and my legs feel weak.

Dane pulls his hand out of my waistband just as the bell chimes and those silver doors open. An older couple stands on the other side. I cannot imagine what I must look like. Dane winks at me, and gestures for me to go first. As I make my way past him, he sticks his fingers in his mouth one by one. He sucks my arousal off of him right in front of the couple. Heat immediately creeps in my cheeks. Not that they know what just happened, but just the thought has me turned on all over again. We need to hurry up and make it to his room before I lose all sanity and fuck him right here in the hallway.

Talk about me doing wild and risky things. I would never! This is so unlike me.

So why am I like this when it comes to Dane?

thirteen

. . .

I waste zero time. The second Dane shuts the door and removes his coat, I jump him. My hands fly to his hair, not caring that I yank his beanie off in the process. I fist his hair while kissing him.

It is my turn to have him.

My hands reach for his sweater, pulling it. I step back just enough to get it over his head then my lips are back on him. I kiss along his collarbone, while my hands work at getting his cargo pants undone. His cock springs free the second I slide both his pants and briefs down. I swear he was not this thick last night.

I swallow down any doubt when I think back to how good the sex was. I can do this. I wrap my hands around his cock and gently guide him to the bed.

The sheets are still a mess. From us, possibly. Or at least I'd like to think they are from us.

With one arm on his chest, I shove him down.

My other hand strokes him while I take in his body. I know I just saw him naked, but if I am being honest, I didn't get to memorize the hard ridges and muscles.

"Callia." Dane grits my name out.

I like the way he says my name. It makes me feel powerful, confident.

I release him and step back. He moans at the loss of contact. I smirk, knowing I have the upper hand right now.

"I want you to watch me," I state so matter of factly.

Dane does as I tell him. He props himself up on his elbows and raises an eyebrow. And damn if his stomach muscles don't stand out.

I slide out of my Uggs while shrugging my coat off. I tease him as I slowly pull my sweatshirt and thermal over my head. Next, my bra comes off and he lets out a hiss. He likes what he sees.

When I take off my snow pants, I do a little twist and bend over, so he gets a view of my ass. Yes, I want to drive him crazy. I want to make him lose control.

And I will.

That is my new goal.

I understand there's a chance this is just a game to him and if that is the case, I can play too.

Now fully naked in front of him, I play with my nipples. Pinching and pulling until I feel myself growing wet. I imagine what it will feel like once I sink down onto his rock-hard cock.

I saunter up to Dane, lean over, and kiss him. His erection tempts me. I could climb on top right now. But where is the fun in that?

I pull back, biting his lips as I go. I grip his cock just before my mouth tightly envelopes it. Dane's hands fly to my hair. I take my time, allowing my tongue to explore. I trace over his veins. I pull back just enough to see that a little bit of pre-cum has pooled at his head. I lick it up ever so slowly before I pull him back into my mouth. I pay extra attention to his head. It's enough to drive him mad. I know this because he lets out a string of curse words. His hand tightens in my hair. I can feel my wetness now between my thighs and I am throbbing. It takes every ounce of self-control to keep myself from climbing on top of Dane. I need him to lose control first.

I need to speed this up because I can hardly wait. My motions pick up as I bob my head up and down. Deciding to be a tad daring, I reach for his balls and squeeze lightly. He nearly bucks me off him while letting out a moan. I can't tell if he likes it or not, so I squeeze again.

"Jesus, Callia, I am going to—"His words drown out as his orgasm takes over.

Warmth hits the back of my throat. I milk every drop from him.

When I am certain he has nothing more to give, I release him and stand up. I smile when I see Dane. His eyes are closed, and he is breathing heavily.

I run my hands up his thighs as I climb to straddle him. His eyes fly open.

"Are you clean?" I ask, wasting no time.

"What?! Yes, why?"

I don't give a reply as I position myself and grip his now semi-hard cock. I lower myself onto him slowly before he can protest. Even though he is not fully erect, he is still thick, and I have to stretch to fit all of him.

He feels good.

"Callia," he warns.

"Hmm?"

"Fuck!" he pants as he grabs my hips.

I continue moving slowly at first. I want this to last however, since we stepped foot into his room, I have been aching with need and feeling him with no barrier has me almost frantic that I cannot get enough.

It does not take long for us to find a rhythm that feels incredible. Dane grips me harder as he guides my movements up and down his cock. It hits me in all the right places, causing that tingling sensation that I have been craving.

Dane must feel it too because his hand slides from my hip down to where our bodies meet. I inhale sharply at his touch. He toys with my clit as the tingling pleasure grows. He flicks and rubs as I begin to move faster. All thoughts of keeping control have melted away at his touch. I crave the way he lights my body ablaze.

This time when I come apart, I scream out his

name, not bothering to care who hears me. I ride the waves until I have nothing left to give. I collapse onto Dane's chest while trying to catch my breath.

When I finally get my mind straight and my heart is no longer racing, I attempt to slide off him, but he holds me in place.

"Are you planning to run again?" he asks, his voice quiet.

Now that I am back to thinking with my brain, reality sets in. I still do not see how this can be much more than just a winter fling. But we just had unprotected sex.

My mind is swirling as I attempt to move. I curl into his side, deciding that I do like how we fit.

If only that could be enough.

Maybe it can be.

"Dane." I pause to try to get my words straight. "I live in Florida, though nowhere near Tampa. How do you think this is actually going to work out between us?" I tap his chest and then point to myself.

"I spend time all over. I teach surf lessons and swim safety in several coastal towns. I teach skiing here. Yes, I have a place back home, but I think we can make this work. Or at least try."

Dane sounds sincere. He truly does. It is just that I am still licking wounds from my ex-boyfriend, Juan.

"I was in a relationship for quite a while, and he cheated. If we do this long-distance thing, I am sure you will be bound to do the same and quite frankly I don't think I am up for any more heartache."

Dane leans up on his elbow. His eyes are practically tiny slits. I must have made him upset.

"I understand that we do not know each other very well, but don't dare compare me to your ex. He's a fucking tool for cheating. A loser, if I might say so. I am nothing like him." He practically grinds that last bit out.

Now I feel bad.

"I am sorry. I should not have compared you to him."

"Give me a chance," he says before laying back down. He starts rubbing little circles along my back. It is soothing. I don't know why, but being here in his arms is soothing.

I make a quick decision right then that I cannot keep living in the past.

Maybe I crave more than his touch.

Maybe I do crave being around him.

fourteen

. . .

I wake suddenly to raised voices. I have no idea what time it is and it takes me a few seconds to take in my surroundings. I am still in Dane's room. That much I know.

The question is, where is he?

Wrapping myself in the white bedsheet, I stand up and follow the voices. I swear they sound like they are coming from the other side of the door. I glance through the peephole to see what is happening.

To my surprise, Dane is standing in the hallway with his ex-girlfriend. He stands there, shirtless, wearing a pair of sweats with his arms crossed. Based on his facial expressions, I'd guess that he is mad. Whatever her name is throws her hands up in the air. It's obvious she's frustrated too.

"I told you, Sasha, we are through. You need to leave."

That's right, her name is Sasha. She must be salty.

"How can you say that? We have so much history."

"We had so much history. Keyword had."

Sasha throws her hands in the air again. "Why are you making this so difficult?"

Dane shakes his head. "Uh, we are no longer a couple, I have asked you several times to leave, so you are the one who is making this difficult."

"Is this because of that dark haired chick that was downstairs with you? It isn't like you and her are even a thing. You would never do such a thing." Sasha jabs her finger into Dane's chest. He stands there, still as a rock. Completely unfazed that she is on the verge of losing her shit.

I, on the other hand, seem to have grown a jealous bone. I do not want her touching him. In fact, I want her to leave.

I yank the door open. There I stand in front of both wrapped in nothing but a white sheet. I am careful to stand in the middle of the doorway so that it doesn't shut and lock me out here. That would be bad. Dane's eyes light up with curiosity while Sasha's grow wide.

"Actually, Dane did such a thing. He did me. Now if you don't mind, I'd like for Dane to come back to bed with me."

Holy shit! Where did that come from?

"Who the hell are you?" she spits out. Her pouting has turned to anger in an instant.

"Callia." I smile and stick my hand out to greet her properly while still holding the white sheet with my other hand. I glance over at Dane. He stands there with amusement on his face.

Sasha glares down at my hand. She doesn't shake it.

"You must be a whore to sleep with some random guy!" she all but screams.

Normally, I would take offense to her words, but seeing as she left Dane because he wasn't dressing the part, her words don't mean shit.

"Says the fake tit blonde who left Dane because he does not wear a suit and tie every day. You should go back home and try to find someone that meets your criteria."

I can hear Dane chuckle over her gasps that are followed by waterworks.

"I can't believe you would do this to us! Why, Dane?!" She is shouting in the hallway now.

"But you did do this. You left him, he found me. End of story," I blurt without thinking. Was that the right thing to say? I look at Dane, who is standing there beaming. He steps past me, snaking his arm around me as he moves.

"Have a safe flight back home," he says before pulling me in and shutting the door.

Her yelling has turned into wails. She is a loud crier. All I can think is thank goodness this is his family's resort, otherwise he would be thrown out. Her too.

Dane drags me to the bed, forcing me to leave all

thoughts of Sasha in the hallway. He pulls the sheet away and climbs over, exposing me to him.

"Did you mean that?" he asks as he starts to kiss and nip my skin.

"Mean what?"

"That I found you. Like you are mine now," he says while his hand slides between my thighs.

Well, when he says it like that and touches me there. Butterflies swirl in my stomach.

"Maybe," I tease.

He places a kiss on my lips. "Maybe? That's all I get?"

He slowly inserts a finger into me while continuing to kiss me. He kisses my lips, my chin. He kisses down my neck until he reaches my breasts. My eyes fall shut as pleasure begins to build.

Dane begins to worship my body in ways that it had never been worshiped before. He touches me in ways that I have never been touched. Only he knows how to make me come apart and then beg for more. And then when he is through ravishing my body, he bathes me and takes care of me in ways that I have only read about in romance books.

I think maybe, just maybe, I can find my own happiness amid this winter fling turned maybe happily ever after.

want more?

If you enjoyed reading about Callia and Dane in A Little Winter Romance, you'll be happy to know that there is more!

Marina and Leon have their own story! A Little Winter Fling is now live!

acknowledgments

Dear Reader,

Thank you for reading A Little Winter Romance. It means the world to me.

Thank you for taking a chance on an indie author. I am forever grateful for your support.

XO,

Lisamarie

about the author

Lisamarie Kade is a romance author living in the Sunshine State with her husband and small army of children.

When not writing, she can be found chasing the kids around or volunteering for one of their many activities.

Lisamarie enjoys chocolate peanut butter cups, music, and reading something steamy while sipping an alcoholic beverage.

also by

The Secrets We Keep

Mended Hearts

The War Within

The Surprise Within

The Christmas Breakdown

Shattered Illusion: The Red Society Book One

Shattered Reality: The Red Society Book Two

www.ingramcontent.com/pod-product-compliance
Lightning Source LLC
Chambersburg PA
CBHW060338310726
48976CB00007B/2608